Wildfire Daily Journal

How to Lead Yourself Well
and Live Out Your Dreams:

A Practical Tool to Daily Focus
Your Life In Gratitude and
Assess Your Order of Priorities

Bill and Stephanie Lammers

Introduction

Thank you for picking up this book! Our hope and prayer is that the Wildfire Daily Journal impacts you deeply and revitalizes the way you pursue your dreams. You might be wondering what "2x5=10" means; it represents five things you are grateful for, your top five priorities, and ten dreams you have for how you want your life to look in ten years. Two times five equals ten. Days make up our years, so clarifying your dreams today lays a solid foundation for ourselves a decade down the road. Why 10 years instead of, for example, 50? If you look too far out, it will be difficult for you to define your dreams and set defined, measurable goals that you can follow through on. At the same time, formulating your dreams ten years in the future gives you time to develop those dreams. We believe that starting each day by listing five things you are thankful for in conjunction with your top five priorities helps you use the right lens to fulfill your dreams for your future. Declaring our dreams every day and intentionally taking daily steps to achieve them helps us focus on our priorities in life, and we believe that it will do the same for you, too.

The Power of an Attitude of Gratitude

Having an attitude of gratitude has deeply affected our lives for the better. What in the world is the big deal with gratitude? Is this just another catchy, trendy thing?

In reality, it's a life-changing thing. We know from personal experience. Almost seven years ago, I (Stephanie) sat on the porch of a small cabin that our family was staying in for a weekend away. I was in the depths of grief. My heart was broken in a million pieces. I was overwhelmed with sadness and I just couldn't seem to get out of the dark place I was in. I was dealing with anxiety and frustration that felt inescapable.

Months before, my dad had passed away unexpectedly. I knew someday my parents would leave this world, but I had absolutely no idea how hard it would hit me in every area of my life. I was working part time and attempting to balance day-to-day life as a wife and mom to four kids. That day, I was sitting in a rocking chair on this little porch, tucked in the middle of the woods, when I heard a still small voice in my heart say, "an attitude of gratitude is **everything**."

I knew at that moment God was prompting me to start each morning with a heart of gratitude. That's when I began the journey of making gratitude a habit. I would write down five things that I was thankful for each and every day. Over time, I recognized that not only was my broken heart healing but my emotions were more at peace, my perspective on life was progressively positive, my physical energy was increasing, and I had a renewed fervor for life again! This small, daily practice made a huge impact. It changed everything, one day at a time.

Are you tired of being overwhelmed in your life, feeling like you're spinning in circles without an ability to sustain in the long run? You're not alone. This may seem like a sales pitch, but I promise you that if you're anything like me, you will not be disappointed with the changes an attitude of gratitude will make in your life.

First thing each morning, write down five things you are thankful for. Instead of worrying about the bill that is due today, the 9 a.m. deadline, or the packed schedule of kids' sports activities, take a moment to pause and recognize five things you are thankful for. It just takes a few seconds and this immediately focuses your mind on the blessings in your life, helping you to approach the day with a positive and productive attitude. That bill may be due today, but you still have the gift of today. That work deadline may seem overwhelming, but you have a paying job.

Gratitude has spiritual, emotional, mental, physical, and social benefits that affect every aspect of your life. Gratitude is scientifically linked to better physical health, higher self-esteem, deeper relationships, improved sleeping patterns, and positive emotions, just to name a few. We all feel the pressures of stress in our lives, and it is both physically and emotionally exhausting. When we are consumed by stress, our thoughts are overwhelmed by the issues, problems, deadlines, etc. that are weighing on us. This quickly exhausts us both physically and emotionally. Our attitude begins to negatively reflect the overwhelming anxiety we feel. However, when we consciously make an effort to direct our thoughts through thankfulness, our perspective radically transforms. Writing down what you are thankful for shifts your focus away from the stress in your life and onto the blessings that are often overlooked.

While there is nothing wrong with brevity when you are recording what you are thankful for, don't be afraid to be specific. Of course you're grateful for your husband, but it will always be more meaningful to write down something more distinct; like you're thankful that he unloaded the dishwasher last night or that he always hugs you when he gets home. Just remember, the important thing is that you continue to journal your thankfulness daily in a way that sets your mind on the positive blessings in your life. Don't simply write the same things each day.

Memorizing the same list of blessings and jotting them down daily will not effectively focus your mind and heart on true gratitude. By being specific and creative each day, you will actually find you have more things to be thankful for than you realized!

Something to keep at the forefront of your mind is that being intentionally thankful affects every area of your life. It doesn't just affect your body or your intellect; it benefits you on a holistic (i.e. whole) level. ***Holistic*** indicates the big picture. When we take a holistic approach, we are looking at our wellbeing as a *whole*. We are all made of three parts, our spirit, body, and soul (our mind, will, and emotions). Having a heart of gratitude has a holistic effect on all three parts of us.

When you live in a state of gratitude, are led by the spirit, your soul (mind & emotions) and body reap the benefits (see illustration). When you practice the art of gratitude, the benefits spread like **wildfire** through every aspect of your life, helping you to forge ahead and live out your dreams.

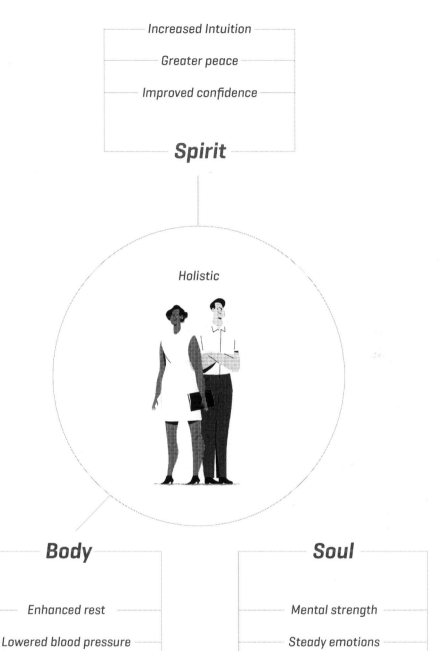

Increased Intuition

Greater peace

Improved confidence

Spirit

Holistic

Body

Enhanced rest

Lowered blood pressure

Boosted energy

Soul

Mental strength

Steady emotions

Improved decision making

5 Constant Priorities

Having the correct order of consistent priorities is crucial to achieving our dreams. If our priorities are out of order, it will be difficult to accomplish our goals because we will be prioritizing distractions that draw our focus away from what truly matters most. Understanding your personal order of priorities is a game-changer. In order to take control of your life and to **intentionally** pursue your dreams, you must understand the order of importance the priorities in your life should be in.

Having the correct order of priorities has been life changing for me (Bill). When I was first married, my priorities were a mess. I put all my energy and focus into my career, working 12 hours a day and 4 hours every Saturday. My top priority was my career and my strive to obtain wealth. Even in the few hours a day I was at home, I was still at work both mentally and emotionally. When our first son Will was born, I even prioritized work and finances over him. I justified this behavior in my mind, telling myself that he was too young to notice. Stephanie was not receiving the love from me that she needed and deserved. As she expressed this to me, I convinced myself that she just didn't understand; after all, I was trying to build wealth *for her*. In reality, I was the one who didn't understand that my life had become consumed with the wrong priorities.

It wasn't until six years into our marriage that I realized just how badly out of order my life had become. At the time, Stephanie was pregnant with our second son (who would be born two weeks later) and we had a wedding out of town to attend that day. It was a rare occasion as I took the day off of work to drive to and attend the wedding. As we arrived at the hotel, I received a phone call to hear the voice of my boss yell,

"Bill, the (manufacturing) plant is on fire!"

"Right" I answered sarcastically, "Tell me what is really going on."

"Seriously! Turn on the news when you get to the hotel. It's burning down!"

I didn't believe him. The first thing I did was turn on the news and watch in shock as the manufacturing plant I had built my life around burned to the ground. That's when it hit me like a boulder. My identity, my career, and my life was contained within that plant. In that moment, I realized how wrong that was.

My wife, my son, and my soon-to be son were alive and safe. They were yearning for a husband and father that loved them deeper than a career or money. I realized that God had not left me, and He longed for a deeper, more intimate relationship with me. I felt terrible. I ran out of the hotel room and escaped back to the car. I locked the doors and wept.

That day changed my life. I realized that my relationship with Christ should be the first priority in my life, followed by my wife, and then my children, my health, finances, and after that my career. I decided that day that I would intentionally live my life according to this order of importance, instead of letting my life dictate what I would prioritize.

As a result, my relationship with Christ has deepened, my marriage is thriving, I have wonderful relationships with my kids, I have a healthier body, and a wonderful career that correctly brings a work/life rhythm.

How can you successfully pursue your dreams if you do not know what you have been putting first in your life, and what *should be* your highest priority? Each day, list your top five priorities in the order they *should* rank in your life, then next to each one circle the number of stars that accurately represents your execution of that priority. The point of this practice is to **filter** your life through your order of priorities and empower you towards **intentional** decision making. Be honest with yourself! The only way you can manage your priorities is by accurately assessing where they stand now.

Define Your Dreams

So, what is a dream? You may not think that you are a dreamer, but the truth is, we *all* have dreams. A dream doesn't have to be something extravagant; it can be something as simple as *I want to be a parent who has thriving relationships with my children.* Dreams are simply wishes and ideas that can be transformed into goals. What do you hope your life will be like in ten years from now? Fill up the next two pages with as many things that come to mind. What job would you like to have? Where would you like to be living? What type of car do you want to be driving? What type of relationships would you like to have in your life? What activities do you wish to be involved in? It's good to be specific with your dreams. Don't limit yourself; let yourself imagine what you really wish your life would be like in a decade.

How I want my life to look in 10 years...

How I want my life to look in 10 years continued...

Wow! Those dreams for your future are amazing! Take a minute to admire the great vision you have for your future. Next, narrow your list down to 10 measurable dreams you have for the future so that you can start declaring those dreams and turning them into goals.

Declaring Your Dreams Until they Come to Pass

Now, write down each dream in present tense on your first journal page. Don't write *I want to be a successful entrepreneur* - instead, write *I am a successful entrepreneur.* "I want to be" is a passive statement. It is as if you are procrastinating on your dream. "I am," however, is a declaration, an announcement of what you are. *I am an entrepreneur.* I may not have invented the light bulb, but *I am an entrepreneur.* State it as a fact. Speaking - and writing - your dreams and goals as a *reality* helps motivate you to live intentionally. If you take a passive approach, hoping without action that someday you will be an entrepreneur, how will you ever become one? Passivity never gets the job done; proactivity moves us steadily towards our goals, no matter how lofty they seem.

It is so important that you declare your dreams out loud. There are scientific studies that reveal how when we speak, our words actually affect us physically. The Bible says that "life and death is in the tongue," and science backs that up in a tangible way. You have so much power in your declarations and it would be a waste to not use that gift to speak life into your future.

Defining and declaring my (Bill) dreams has been revolutionary for me. I would struggle with the same things repeatedly (exercise, perfectionism, etc.) but by implementing the 2x5=10 process every morning, it has revealed and exposed things that were holding me back. It has challenged me to have strategic thinking versus random thinking. And it has allowed me to stay focused on incremental steps of progress. The process helps me focus on the course of what I want my life to look like in 10 years and I don't feel discouraged and defeated when I haven't conquered it all in one month.

Focusing on your blessings and filtering life through your priorities will help you to live intentionally to achieve your dreams. It is important to note that your dreams will be refined or may even completely change as you continue to declare them verbally and in writing. That is okay! The important thing is that you know the direction you want to go, and that you are living intentionally to achieve those goals. Each day at the bottom of your journal page is a "The Next Step I Will Take Today" section. This is for you to decide one or two actions you will do that day to take the next step closer to completing your dreams. Use it to hold yourself accountable to living **intentionally**. You will find that it is encouraging to look back and be able to note that you took a certain action, no matter how small, towards your goals. We attain our dreams step by step and every step is a victory. This is our heart, and we hope it becomes yours as well:

> "I don't know about you, but I'm running hard for the finish line. I'm giving it everything I've got. No sloppy living for me! I'm staying alert and in top condition. I'm not going to get caught napping, telling everyone else all about it and then missing out myself."
>
> ~ 1 Corinthians 9:26-27 (MSG)

We encourage you to daily complete the 2x5=10; five things you are grateful for, your top five priorities, and ten dreams you have for how you want your life to look in ten years.

Start running toward your dreams today!

God bless you on this journey!
Bill and Stephanie

Today's Date 9-19-19

Jerry Smith

Today I'm Grateful For	Order of Priorities	How did I do Yesterday?
1. Clean drinking water	1. Relationship with Christ	★ ★ ★ ★ ☆
2. Working vehicle to drive to work	2. My Wife	★ ★ ★ ☆ ☆
3. Kids that do not do drugs	3. My Kids	★ ★ ★ ★ ★
4. Time to watch basketball	4. Health / Exercise	★ ★ ★ ★ ★
5. A wife who encourages me	5. Work	★ ☆ ☆ ☆ ☆

Ten Dreams / Declarations:

1. I am a great dad that encourages my kids to pursue their passions

2. I am a husband that brings joy to my wife daily

3. I am an entrepreneur with a product patent

4. I am a published author of 2 books

5. I am a high school basketball coach with a winning record

6. We built our own house

7. I sing on the church worship team

8. We took a family trip to see the Grand Canyon

9. I got promoted to managing partner

10. We adopted a child from Africa

The next step(s) I am taking today
I will surprise my wife by leaving a note of appreciation for her. I will apply for open basketball coach positions.

Today I'm Grateful For	Order of Priorities	How did I do Yesterday?
1.	1.	☆ ☆ ☆ ☆ ☆
2.	2.	☆ ☆ ☆ ☆ ☆
3.	3.	☆ ☆ ☆ ☆ ☆
4.	4.	☆ ☆ ☆ ☆ ☆
5.	5.	☆ ☆ ☆ ☆ ☆

Ten Dreams / Declarations:

1.

2.

3.

4.

5.

6.

7.

8.

9.

10.

The next step(s) I am taking today

Today's Date

Today I'm Grateful For

1.
2.
3.
4.
5.

Order of Priorities

1.
2.
3.
4.
5.

How did I do Yesterday?

☆ ☆ ☆ ☆ ☆
☆ ☆ ☆ ☆ ☆
☆ ☆ ☆ ☆ ☆
☆ ☆ ☆ ☆ ☆
☆ ☆ ☆ ☆ ☆

Ten Dreams / Declarations:

1.
2.
3.
4.
5.
6.
7.
8.
9.
10.

The next step(s) I am taking today

Today I'm Grateful For	Order of Priorities	How did I do Yesterday?
1.	1.	☆ ☆ ☆ ☆ ☆
2.	2.	☆ ☆ ☆ ☆ ☆
3.	3.	☆ ☆ ☆ ☆ ☆
4.	4.	☆ ☆ ☆ ☆ ☆
5.	5.	☆ ☆ ☆ ☆ ☆

Ten Dreams / Declarations:

1.

2.

3.

4.

5.

6.

7.

8.

9.

10.

The next step(s) I am taking today

Today's Date

Today I'm Grateful For

1.

2.

3.

4.

5.

Order of Priorities

1.

2.

3.

4.

5.

How did I do Yesterday?

☆ ☆ ☆ ☆ ☆

☆ ☆ ☆ ☆ ☆

☆ ☆ ☆ ☆ ☆

☆ ☆ ☆ ☆ ☆

☆ ☆ ☆ ☆ ☆

Ten Dreams / Declarations:

1.

2.

3.

4.

5.

6.

7.

8.

9.

10.

The next step(s) I am taking today

Today I'm Grateful For

1.
2.
3.
4.
5.

Order of Priorities

1.
2.
3.
4.
5.

How did I do Yesterday?

☆ ☆ ☆ ☆ ☆
☆ ☆ ☆ ☆ ☆
☆ ☆ ☆ ☆ ☆
☆ ☆ ☆ ☆ ☆
☆ ☆ ☆ ☆ ☆

Ten Dreams / Declarations:

1.
2.
3.
4.
5.
6.
7.
8.
9.
10.

The next step(s) I am taking today

Today's Date

Today I'm Grateful For

1.
2.
3.
4.
5.

Order of Priorities

1.
2.
3.
4.
5.

☆ ☆ ☆ ☆ ☆
☆ ☆ ☆ ☆ ☆
☆ ☆ ☆ ☆ ☆
☆ ☆ ☆ ☆ ☆
☆ ☆ ☆ ☆ ☆

Ten Dreams / Declarations:

1.
2.
3.
4.
5.
6.
7.
8.
9.
10.

The next step(s) I am taking today

Today I'm Grateful For	Order of Priorities	How did I do Yesterday?
1.	1.	☆ ☆ ☆ ☆ ☆
2.	2.	☆ ☆ ☆ ☆ ☆
3.	3.	☆ ☆ ☆ ☆ ☆
4.	4.	☆ ☆ ☆ ☆ ☆
5.	5.	☆ ☆ ☆ ☆ ☆

Ten Dreams / Declarations:

1.

2.

3.

4.

5.

6.

7.

8.

9.

10.

The next step(s) I am taking today

Today I'm Grateful For

1.

2.

3.

4.

5.

Order of Priorities

1.

2.

3.

4.

5.

How did I do Yesterday?

☆ ☆ ☆ ☆ ☆

☆ ☆ ☆ ☆ ☆

☆ ☆ ☆ ☆ ☆

☆ ☆ ☆ ☆ ☆

☆ ☆ ☆ ☆ ☆

Ten Dreams / Declarations:

1.

2.

3.

4.

5.

6.

7.

8.

9.

10.

The next step[s] I am taking today

Today I'm Grateful For	Order of Priorities	How did I do Yesterday?
1.	1.	☆ ☆ ☆ ☆ ☆
2.	2.	☆ ☆ ☆ ☆ ☆
3.	3.	☆ ☆ ☆ ☆ ☆
4.	4.	☆ ☆ ☆ ☆ ☆
5.	5.	☆ ☆ ☆ ☆ ☆

Ten Dreams / Declarations:

1.

2.

3.

4.

5.

6.

7.

8.

9.

10.

The next step(s) I am taking today

Today I'm Grateful For

1.
2.
3.
4.
5.

Order of Priorities

1.
2.
3.
4.
5.

How did I do Yesterday?

☆ ☆ ☆ ☆ ☆
☆ ☆ ☆ ☆ ☆
☆ ☆ ☆ ☆ ☆
☆ ☆ ☆ ☆ ☆
☆ ☆ ☆ ☆ ☆

Ten Dreams / Declarations:

1.

2.

3.

4.

5.

6.

7.

8.

9.

10.

The next step(s) I am taking today

Today I'm Grateful For	Order of Priorities	How did I do Yesterday?
1.	1.	☆ ☆ ☆ ☆ ☆
2.	2.	☆ ☆ ☆ ☆ ☆
3.	3.	☆ ☆ ☆ ☆ ☆
4.	4.	☆ ☆ ☆ ☆ ☆
5.	5.	☆ ☆ ☆ ☆ ☆

Ten Dreams / Declarations:

1.

2.

3.

4.

5.

6.

7.

8.

9.

10.

The next step(s) I am taking today

Today's Date

Today I'm Grateful For

1.

2.

3.

4.

5.

Order of Priorities

1.

2.

3.

4.

5.

How did I do Yesterday?

☆ ☆ ☆ ☆ ☆

☆ ☆ ☆ ☆ ☆

☆ ☆ ☆ ☆ ☆

☆ ☆ ☆ ☆ ☆

☆ ☆ ☆ ☆ ☆

Ten Dreams / Declarations:

1.

2.

3.

4.

5.

6.

7.

8.

9.

10.

The next step(s) I am taking today

Today's Date

Today I'm Grateful For	Order of Priorities	How did I do Yesterday?
1.	1.	☆ ☆ ☆ ☆ ☆
2.	2.	☆ ☆ ☆ ☆ ☆
3.	3.	☆ ☆ ☆ ☆ ☆
4.	4.	☆ ☆ ☆ ☆ ☆
5.	5.	☆ ☆ ☆ ☆ ☆

Ten Dreams / Declarations:

1.

2.

3.

4.

5.

6.

7.

8.

9.

10.

The next step(s) I am taking today

Today I'm Grateful For

1.
2.
3.
4.
5.

Order of Priorities

1.
2.
3.
4.
5.

How did I do Yesterday?

☆ ☆ ☆ ☆ ☆
☆ ☆ ☆ ☆ ☆
☆ ☆ ☆ ☆ ☆
☆ ☆ ☆ ☆ ☆
☆ ☆ ☆ ☆ ☆

Ten Dreams / Declarations:

1.

2.

3.

4.

5.

6.

7.

8.

9.

10.

The next step(s) I am taking today

Today's Date

Today I'm Grateful For	Order of Priorities	How did I do Yesterday?
1.	1.	☆ ☆ ☆ ☆ ☆
2.	2.	☆ ☆ ☆ ☆ ☆
3.	3.	☆ ☆ ☆ ☆ ☆
4.	4.	☆ ☆ ☆ ☆ ☆
5.	5.	☆ ☆ ☆ ☆ ☆

Ten Dreams / Declarations:

1.

2.

3.

4.

5.

6.

7.

8.

9.

10.

The next step(s) I am taking today

Today's Date

Today I'm Grateful For

1.

2.

3.

4.

5.

Order of Priorities

1.

2.

3.

4.

5.

How did I do Yesterday?

☆ ☆ ☆ ☆ ☆

☆ ☆ ☆ ☆ ☆

☆ ☆ ☆ ☆ ☆

☆ ☆ ☆ ☆ ☆

☆ ☆ ☆ ☆ ☆

Ten Dreams / Declarations:

1.

2.

3.

4.

5.

6.

7.

8.

9.

10.

The next step(s) I am taking today

Today's Date

Today I'm Grateful For	Order of Priorities	How did I do Yesterday?
1.	1.	☆ ☆ ☆ ☆ ☆
2.	2.	☆ ☆ ☆ ☆ ☆
3.	3.	☆ ☆ ☆ ☆ ☆
4.	4.	☆ ☆ ☆ ☆ ☆
5.	5.	☆ ☆ ☆ ☆ ☆

Ten Dreams / Declarations:

1.

2.

3.

4.

5.

6.

7.

8.

9.

10.

The next step(s) I am taking today

Today I'm Grateful For

1.

2.

3.

4.

5.

Order of Priorities

1.

2.

3.

4.

5.

How did I do Yesterday?

☆ ☆ ☆ ☆ ☆

☆ ☆ ☆ ☆ ☆

☆ ☆ ☆ ☆ ☆

☆ ☆ ☆ ☆ ☆

☆ ☆ ☆ ☆ ☆

Ten Dreams / Declarations:

1.

2.

3.

4.

5.

6.

7.

8.

9.

10.

The next step(s) I am taking today

Today's Date

Today I'm Grateful For	Order of Priorities	How did I do Yesterday?
1.	1.	☆ ☆ ☆ ☆ ☆
2.	2.	☆ ☆ ☆ ☆ ☆
3.	3.	☆ ☆ ☆ ☆ ☆
4.	4.	☆ ☆ ☆ ☆ ☆
5.	5.	☆ ☆ ☆ ☆ ☆

Ten Dreams / Declarations:

1.

2.

3.

4.

5.

6.

7.

8.

9.

10.

The next step(s) I am taking today

Today's Date

Today I'm Grateful For

1.
2.
3.
4.
5.

Order of Priorities

1.
2.
3.
4.
5.

How did I do Yesterday?

☆ ☆ ☆ ☆ ☆
☆ ☆ ☆ ☆ ☆
☆ ☆ ☆ ☆ ☆
☆ ☆ ☆ ☆ ☆
☆ ☆ ☆ ☆ ☆

Ten Dreams / Declarations:

1.

2.

3.

4.

5.

6.

7.

8.

9.

10.

The next step(s) I am taking today

Today's Date

Today I'm Grateful For	Order of Priorities	How did I do Yesterday?

Today I'm Grateful For

1.

2.

3.

4.

5.

Order of Priorities

1. ☆ ☆ ☆ ☆ ☆

2. ☆ ☆ ☆ ☆ ☆

3. ☆ ☆ ☆ ☆ ☆

4. ☆ ☆ ☆ ☆ ☆

5. ☆ ☆ ☆ ☆ ☆

Ten Dreams / Declarations:

1.

2.

3.

4.

5.

6.

7.

8.

9.

10.

The next step(s) I am taking today

Today I'm Grateful For	Order of Priorities	How did I do Yesterday?
1.	1.	☆ ☆ ☆ ☆ ☆
2.	2.	☆ ☆ ☆ ☆ ☆
3.	3.	☆ ☆ ☆ ☆ ☆
4.	4.	☆ ☆ ☆ ☆ ☆
5.	5.	☆ ☆ ☆ ☆ ☆

Ten Dreams / Declarations:

1.

2.

3.

4.

5.

6.

7.

8.

9.

10.

The next step(s) I am taking today

Today I'm Grateful For	Order of Priorities	How did I do Yesterday?
1.	1.	☆ ☆ ☆ ☆ ☆
2.	2.	☆ ☆ ☆ ☆ ☆
3.	3.	☆ ☆ ☆ ☆ ☆
4.	4.	☆ ☆ ☆ ☆ ☆
5.	5.	☆ ☆ ☆ ☆ ☆

Ten Dreams / Declarations:

1.

2.

3.

4.

5.

6.

7.

8.

9.

10.

The next step[s] I am taking today

Today I'm Grateful For

1.
2.
3.
4.
5.

Order of Priorities

1.
2.
3.
4.
5.

How did I do Yesterday?

☆ ☆ ☆ ☆ ☆
☆ ☆ ☆ ☆ ☆
☆ ☆ ☆ ☆ ☆
☆ ☆ ☆ ☆ ☆
☆ ☆ ☆ ☆ ☆

Ten Dreams / Declarations:

1.

2.

3.

4.

5.

6.

7.

8.

9.

10.

The next step(s) I am taking today

Today's Date

Today I'm Grateful For

1.
2.
3.
4.
5.

Order of Priorities

1.
2.
3.
4.
5.

How did I do Yesterday?

☆ ☆ ☆ ☆ ☆
☆ ☆ ☆ ☆ ☆
☆ ☆ ☆ ☆ ☆
☆ ☆ ☆ ☆ ☆
☆ ☆ ☆ ☆ ☆

Ten Dreams / Declarations:

1.
2.
3.
4.
5.
6.
7.
8.
9.
10.

The next step(s) I am taking today

Today's Date

Today I'm Grateful For

1.

2.

3.

4.

5.

Order of Priorities

1.

2.

3.

4.

5.

How did I do Yesterday?

☆ ☆ ☆ ☆ ☆

☆ ☆ ☆ ☆ ☆

☆ ☆ ☆ ☆ ☆

☆ ☆ ☆ ☆ ☆

☆ ☆ ☆ ☆ ☆

Ten Dreams / Declarations:

1.

2.

3.

4.

5.

6.

7.

8.

9.

10.

The next step(s) I am taking today

Today's Date

Today I'm Grateful For	Order of Priorities	How did I do Yesterday?
1.	1.	☆ ☆ ☆ ☆ ☆
2.	2.	☆ ☆ ☆ ☆ ☆
3.	3.	☆ ☆ ☆ ☆ ☆
4.	4.	☆ ☆ ☆ ☆ ☆
5.	5.	☆ ☆ ☆ ☆ ☆

Ten Dreams / Declarations:

1.

2.

3.

4.

5.

6.

7.

8.

9.

10.

The next step[s] I am taking today

Today I'm Grateful For

1.

2.

3.

4.

5.

Order of Priorities

1.

2.

3.

4.

5.

How did I do Yesterday?

☆ ☆ ☆ ☆ ☆

☆ ☆ ☆ ☆ ☆

☆ ☆ ☆ ☆ ☆

☆ ☆ ☆ ☆ ☆

☆ ☆ ☆ ☆ ☆

Ten Dreams / Declarations:

1.

2.

3.

4.

5.

6.

7.

8.

9.

10.

The next step(s) I am taking today

Today I'm Grateful For

1.

2.

3.

4.

5.

Order of Priorities

1.

2.

3.

4.

5.

How did I do Yesterday?

☆ ☆ ☆ ☆ ☆

☆ ☆ ☆ ☆ ☆

☆ ☆ ☆ ☆ ☆

☆ ☆ ☆ ☆ ☆

☆ ☆ ☆ ☆ ☆

Ten Dreams / Declarations:

1.

2.

3.

4.

5.

6.

7.

8.

9.

10.

The next step(s) I am taking today

Today's Date

Today I'm Grateful For

1.
2.
3.
4.
5.

Order of Priorities

1.
2.
3.
4.
5.

How did I do Yesterday?

☆ ☆ ☆ ☆ ☆
☆ ☆ ☆ ☆ ☆
☆ ☆ ☆ ☆ ☆
☆ ☆ ☆ ☆ ☆
☆ ☆ ☆ ☆ ☆

Ten Dreams / Declarations:

1.
2.
3.
4.
5.
6.
7.
8.
9.
10.

The next step(s) I am taking today

Today's Date

Today I'm Grateful For	Order of Priorities	How did I do Yesterday?
1.	1.	☆ ☆ ☆ ☆ ☆
2.	2.	☆ ☆ ☆ ☆ ☆
3.	3.	☆ ☆ ☆ ☆ ☆
4.	4.	☆ ☆ ☆ ☆ ☆
5.	5.	☆ ☆ ☆ ☆ ☆

Ten Dreams / Declarations:

1.

2.

3.

4.

5.

6.

7.

8.

9.

10.

The next step(s) I am taking today

Today's Date

Today I'm Grateful For

1.
2.
3.
4.
5.

Order of Priorities

1.
2.
3.
4.
5.

How did I do Yesterday?

☆ ☆ ☆ ☆ ☆
☆ ☆ ☆ ☆ ☆
☆ ☆ ☆ ☆ ☆
☆ ☆ ☆ ☆ ☆
☆ ☆ ☆ ☆ ☆

Ten Dreams / Declarations:

1.
2.
3.
4.
5.
6.
7.
8.
9.
10.

The next step[s] I am taking today

Today I'm Grateful For

1.

2.

3.

4.

5.

Order of Priorities

1.

2.

3.

4.

5.

How did I do Yesterday?

☆ ☆ ☆ ☆ ☆

☆ ☆ ☆ ☆ ☆

☆ ☆ ☆ ☆ ☆

☆ ☆ ☆ ☆ ☆

☆ ☆ ☆ ☆ ☆

Ten Dreams / Declarations:

1.

2.

3.

4.

5.

6.

7.

8.

9.

10.

The next step(s) I am taking today

Today's Date

Today I'm Grateful For

1.

2.

3.

4.

5.

Order of Priorities

1.

2.

3.

4.

5.

How did I do Yesterday?

☆ ☆ ☆ ☆ ☆

☆ ☆ ☆ ☆ ☆

☆ ☆ ☆ ☆ ☆

☆ ☆ ☆ ☆ ☆

☆ ☆ ☆ ☆ ☆

Ten Dreams / Declarations:

1.

2.

3.

4.

5.

6.

7.

.8.

9.

10.

The next step(s) I am taking today

Today I'm Grateful For	Order of Priorities	How did I do Yesterday?
1.	1.	☆ ☆ ☆ ☆ ☆
2.	2.	☆ ☆ ☆ ☆ ☆
3.	3.	☆ ☆ ☆ ☆ ☆
4.	4.	☆ ☆ ☆ ☆ ☆
5.	5.	☆ ☆ ☆ ☆ ☆

Ten Dreams / Declarations:

1.

2.

3.

4.

5.

6.

7.

8.

9.

10.

The next step(s) I am taking today

Today's Date

Today I'm Grateful For

1.
2.
3.
4.
5.

Order of Priorities

1.
2.
3.
4.
5.

How did I do Yesterday?

☆ ☆ ☆ ☆ ☆
☆ ☆ ☆ ☆ ☆
☆ ☆ ☆ ☆ ☆
☆ ☆ ☆ ☆ ☆
☆ ☆ ☆ ☆ ☆

Ten Dreams / Declarations:

1.

2.

3.

4.

5.

6.

7.

8.

9.

10.

The next step(s) I am taking today

Today I'm Grateful For

Order of Priorities

1.

1. ☆ ☆ ☆ ☆ ☆

2.

2. ☆ ☆ ☆ ☆ ☆

3.

3. ☆ ☆ ☆ ☆ ☆

4.

4. ☆ ☆ ☆ ☆ ☆

5.

5. ☆ ☆ ☆ ☆ ☆

Ten Dreams / Declarations:

1.

2.

3.

4.

5.

6.

7.

8.

9.

10.

The next step[s] I am taking today

Today I'm Grateful For

1.
2.
3.
4.
5.

Order of Priorities

1.
2.
3.
4.
5.

How did I do Yesterday?

☆ ☆ ☆ ☆ ☆
☆ ☆ ☆ ☆ ☆
☆ ☆ ☆ ☆ ☆
☆ ☆ ☆ ☆ ☆
☆ ☆ ☆ ☆ ☆

Ten Dreams / Declarations:

1.
2.
3.
4.
5.
6.
7.
8.
9.
10.

The next step[s] I am taking today

Today I'm Grateful For	Order of Priorities	How did I do Yesterday?
1.	1.	☆ ☆ ☆ ☆ ☆
2.	2.	☆ ☆ ☆ ☆ ☆
3.	3.	☆ ☆ ☆ ☆ ☆
4.	4.	☆ ☆ ☆ ☆ ☆
5.	5.	☆ ☆ ☆ ☆ ☆

Ten Dreams / Declarations:

1.

2.

3.

4.

5.

6.

7.

8.

9.

10.

The next step(s) I am taking today

Today's Date

Today I'm Grateful For

1.

2.

3.

4.

5.

Order of Priorities

1.

2.

3.

4.

5.

How did I do Yesterday?

☆ ☆ ☆ ☆ ☆

☆ ☆ ☆ ☆ ☆

☆ ☆ ☆ ☆ ☆

☆ ☆ ☆ ☆ ☆

☆ ☆ ☆ ☆ ☆

Ten Dreams / Declarations:

1.

2.

3.

4.

5.

6.

7.

8.

9.

10.

The next step(s) I am taking today

Today I'm Grateful For	Order of Priorities	How did I do Yesterday?
1.	1.	☆ ☆ ☆ ☆ ☆
2.	2.	☆ ☆ ☆ ☆ ☆
3.	3.	☆ ☆ ☆ ☆ ☆
4.	4.	☆ ☆ ☆ ☆ ☆
5.	5.	☆ ☆ ☆ ☆ ☆

Ten Dreams / Declarations:

1.

2.

3.

4.

5.

6.

7.

8.

9.

10.

The next step(s) I am taking today

Today's Date

Today I'm Grateful For	Order of Priorities	How did I do Yesterday?

Today I'm Grateful For

1.

2.

3.

4.

5.

Order of Priorities

1. ☆ ☆ ☆ ☆ ☆

2. ☆ ☆ ☆ ☆ ☆

3. ☆ ☆ ☆ ☆ ☆

4. ☆ ☆ ☆ ☆ ☆

5. ☆ ☆ ☆ ☆ ☆

Ten Dreams / Declarations:

1.

2.

3.

4.

5.

6.

7.

8.

9.

10.

The next step(s) I am taking today

Today I'm Grateful For	Order of Priorities	How did I do Yesterday?
1.	1.	☆ ☆ ☆ ☆ ☆
2.	2.	☆ ☆ ☆ ☆ ☆
3.	3.	☆ ☆ ☆ ☆ ☆
4.	4.	☆ ☆ ☆ ☆ ☆
5.	5.	☆ ☆ ☆ ☆ ☆

Ten Dreams / Declarations:

1.

2.

3.

4.

5.

6.

7.

8.

9.

10.

The next step(s) I am taking today

Today's Date

Today I'm Grateful For

1.

2.

3.

4.

5.

Order of Priorities

1.

2.

3.

4.

5.

How did I
do Yesterday?

☆ ☆ ☆ ☆ ☆

☆ ☆ ☆ ☆ ☆

☆ ☆ ☆ ☆ ☆

☆ ☆ ☆ ☆ ☆

☆ ☆ ☆ ☆ ☆

Ten Dreams / Declarations:

1.

2.

3.

4.

5.

6.

7.

8.

9.

10.

The next step(s) I am taking today

Today I'm Grateful For

1.

2.

3.

4.

5.

Order of Priorities

1.

2.

3.

4.

5.

How did I
do Yesterday?

☆ ☆ ☆ ☆ ☆

☆ ☆ ☆ ☆ ☆

☆ ☆ ☆ ☆ ☆

☆ ☆ ☆ ☆ ☆

☆ ☆ ☆ ☆ ☆

Ten Dreams / Declarations:

1.

2.

3.

4.

5.

6.

7.

8.

9.

10.

The next step(s) I am taking today

Today's Date

Today I'm Grateful For

1.
2.
3.
4.
5.

Order of Priorities	How did I do Yesterday?
1.	☆ ☆ ☆ ☆ ☆
2.	☆ ☆ ☆ ☆ ☆
3.	☆ ☆ ☆ ☆ ☆
4.	☆ ☆ ☆ ☆ ☆
5.	☆ ☆ ☆ ☆ ☆

Ten Dreams / Declarations:

1.

2.

3.

4.

5.

6.

7.

8.

9.

10.

The next step(s) I am taking today

Today I'm Grateful For

1.

2.

3.

4.

5.

Order of Priorities

1.

2.

3.

4.

5.

How did I do Yesterday?

☆ ☆ ☆ ☆ ☆

☆ ☆ ☆ ☆ ☆

☆ ☆ ☆ ☆ ☆

☆ ☆ ☆ ☆ ☆

☆ ☆ ☆ ☆ ☆

Ten Dreams / Declarations:

1.

2.

3.

4.

5.

6.

7.

8.

9.

10.

The next step(s) I am taking today

Today's Date

Today I'm Grateful For

1.
2.
3.
4.
5.

Order of Priorities

1.
2.
3.
4.
5.

How did I do Yesterday?

☆ ☆ ☆ ☆ ☆
☆ ☆ ☆ ☆ ☆
☆ ☆ ☆ ☆ ☆
☆ ☆ ☆ ☆ ☆
☆ ☆ ☆ ☆ ☆

Ten Dreams / Declarations:

1.
2.
3.
4.
5.
6.
7.
8.
9.
10.

The next step(s) I am taking today

Today I'm Grateful For	Order of Priorities	How did I do Yesterday?
1.	1.	☆ ☆ ☆ ☆ ☆
2.	2.	☆ ☆ ☆ ☆ ☆
3.	3.	☆ ☆ ☆ ☆ ☆
4.	4.	☆ ☆ ☆ ☆ ☆
5.	5.	☆ ☆ ☆ ☆ ☆

Ten Dreams / Declarations:

1.

2.

3.

4.

5.

6.

7.

8.

9.

10.

The next step(s) I am taking today

Today I'm Grateful For

1.
2.
3.
4.
5.

Order of Priorities

1.
2.
3.
4.
5.

How did I do Yesterday?

☆ ☆ ☆ ☆ ☆
☆ ☆ ☆ ☆ ☆
☆ ☆ ☆ ☆ ☆
☆ ☆ ☆ ☆ ☆
☆ ☆ ☆ ☆ ☆

Ten Dreams / Declarations:

1.

2.

3.

4.

5.

6.

7.

8.

9.

10.

The next step[s] I am taking today

Today I'm Grateful For	Order of Priorities	How did I do Yesterday?
1.	1.	☆ ☆ ☆ ☆ ☆
2.	2.	☆ ☆ ☆ ☆ ☆
3.	3.	☆ ☆ ☆ ☆ ☆
4.	4.	☆ ☆ ☆ ☆ ☆
5.	5.	☆ ☆ ☆ ☆ ☆

Ten Dreams / Declarations:

1.

2.

3.

4.

5.

6.

7.

8.

9.

10.

The next step(s) I am taking today

Today I'm Grateful For

1.
2.
3.
4.
5.

Order of Priorities

1.
2.
3.
4.
5.

How did I do Yesterday?

☆ ☆ ☆ ☆ ☆
☆ ☆ ☆ ☆ ☆
☆ ☆ ☆ ☆ ☆
☆ ☆ ☆ ☆ ☆
☆ ☆ ☆ ☆ ☆

Ten Dreams / Declarations:

1.
2.
3.
4.
5.
6.
7.
8.
9.
10.

The next step(s) I am taking today

Today I'm Grateful For	Order of Priorities	How did I do Yesterday?
1.	1.	☆ ☆ ☆ ☆ ☆
2.	2.	☆ ☆ ☆ ☆ ☆
3.	3.	☆ ☆ ☆ ☆ ☆
4.	4.	☆ ☆ ☆ ☆ ☆
5.	5.	☆ ☆ ☆ ☆ ☆

Ten Dreams / Declarations:

1.

2.

3.

4.

5.

6.

7.

8.

9.

10.

The next step(s) I am taking today

Today's Date

Today I'm Grateful For	Order of Priorities	How did I do Yesterday?
1.	1.	☆ ☆ ☆ ☆ ☆
2.	2.	☆ ☆ ☆ ☆ ☆
3.	3.	☆ ☆ ☆ ☆ ☆
4.	4.	☆ ☆ ☆ ☆ ☆
5.	5.	☆ ☆ ☆ ☆ ☆

Ten Dreams / Declarations:

1.

2.

3.

4.

5.

6.

7.

8.

9.

10.

The next step(s) I am taking today

Today's Date

Today I'm Grateful For

1.

2.

3.

4.

5.

Order of Priorities

1.

2.

3.

4.

5.

How did I do Yesterday?

☆ ☆ ☆ ☆ ☆

☆ ☆ ☆ ☆ ☆

☆ ☆ ☆ ☆ ☆

☆ ☆ ☆ ☆ ☆

☆ ☆ ☆ ☆ ☆

Ten Dreams / Declarations:

1.

2.

3.

4.

5.

6.

7.

8.

9.

10.

The next step(s) I am taking today

Today I'm Grateful For

1.

2.

3.

4.

5.

Order of Priorities

1.

2.

3.

4.

5.

How did I do Yesterday?

☆ ☆ ☆ ☆ ☆

☆ ☆ ☆ ☆ ☆

☆ ☆ ☆ ☆ ☆

☆ ☆ ☆ ☆ ☆

☆ ☆ ☆ ☆ ☆

Ten Dreams / Declarations:

1.

2.

3.

4.

5.

6.

7.

8.

9.

10.

The next step(s) I am taking today

Today I'm Grateful For

1.
2.
3.
4.
5.

Order of Priorities

1.
2.
3.
4.
5.

How did I do Yesterday?

☆ ☆ ☆ ☆ ☆
☆ ☆ ☆ ☆ ☆
☆ ☆ ☆ ☆ ☆
☆ ☆ ☆ ☆ ☆
☆ ☆ ☆ ☆ ☆

Ten Dreams / Declarations:

1.
2.
3.
4.
5.
6.
7.
8.
9.
10.

The next step(s) I am taking today

Today I'm Grateful For

Order of Priorities

1.   1.   ☆ ☆ ☆ ☆ ☆

2.   2.   ☆ ☆ ☆ ☆ ☆

3.   3.   ☆ ☆ ☆ ☆ ☆

4.   4.   ☆ ☆ ☆ ☆ ☆

5.   5.   ☆ ☆ ☆ ☆ ☆

Ten Dreams / Declarations:

1.

2.

3.

4.

5.

6.

7.

8.

9.

10.

The next step(s) I am taking today

Today I'm Grateful For	Order of Priorities	How did I do Yesterday?
1.	1.	☆ ☆ ☆ ☆ ☆
2.	2.	☆ ☆ ☆ ☆ ☆
3.	3.	☆ ☆ ☆ ☆ ☆
4.	4.	☆ ☆ ☆ ☆ ☆
5.	5.	☆ ☆ ☆ ☆ ☆

Ten Dreams / Declarations:

1.

2.

3.

4.

5.

6.

7.

8.

9.

10.

The next step(s) I am taking today

Today I'm Grateful For

1.

2.

3.

4.

5.

Order of Priorities

1.

2.

3.

4.

5.

How did I do Yesterday?

☆ ☆ ☆ ☆ ☆

☆ ☆ ☆ ☆ ☆

☆ ☆ ☆ ☆ ☆

☆ ☆ ☆ ☆ ☆

☆ ☆ ☆ ☆ ☆

Ten Dreams / Declarations:

1.

2.

3.

4.

5.

6.

7.

8.

9.

10.

The next step(s) I am taking today

Today I'm Grateful For

1.
2.
3.
4.
5.

Order of Priorities

1.
2.
3.
4.
5.

How did I do Yesterday?

☆ ☆ ☆ ☆ ☆
☆ ☆ ☆ ☆ ☆
☆ ☆ ☆ ☆ ☆
☆ ☆ ☆ ☆ ☆
☆ ☆ ☆ ☆ ☆

Ten Dreams / Declarations:

1.

2.

3.

4.

5.

6.

7.

8.

9.

10.

The next step(s) I am taking today

Today I'm Grateful For

1.

2.

3.

4.

5.

Order of Priorities

1.

2.

3.

4.

5.

How did I do Yesterday?

☆ ☆ ☆ ☆ ☆

☆ ☆ ☆ ☆ ☆

☆ ☆ ☆ ☆ ☆

☆ ☆ ☆ ☆ ☆

☆ ☆ ☆ ☆ ☆

Ten Dreams / Declarations:

1.

2.

3.

4.

5.

6.

7.

8.

9.

10.

The next step(s) I am taking today

Today I'm Grateful For

1.

2.

3.

4.

5.

Order of Priorities

1.

2.

3.

4.

5.

How did I do Yesterday?

☆ ☆ ☆ ☆ ☆

☆ ☆ ☆ ☆ ☆

☆ ☆ ☆ ☆ ☆

☆ ☆ ☆ ☆ ☆

☆ ☆ ☆ ☆ ☆

Ten Dreams / Declarations:

1.

2.

3.

4.

5.

6.

7.

8.

9.

10.

The next step(s) I am taking today

Today's Date

Today I'm Grateful For	Order of Priorities	How did I do Yesterday?
1.	1.	☆ ☆ ☆ ☆ ☆
2.	2.	☆ ☆ ☆ ☆ ☆
3.	3.	☆ ☆ ☆ ☆ ☆
4.	4.	☆ ☆ ☆ ☆ ☆
5.	5.	☆ ☆ ☆ ☆ ☆

Ten Dreams / Declarations:

1.

2.

3.

4.

5.

6.

7.

8.

9.

10.

The next step(s) I am taking today

Today I'm Grateful For

1.
2.
3.
4.
5.

Order of Priorities

1.
2.
3.
4.
5.

How did I do Yesterday?

☆ ☆ ☆ ☆ ☆
☆ ☆ ☆ ☆ ☆
☆ ☆ ☆ ☆ ☆
☆ ☆ ☆ ☆ ☆
☆ ☆ ☆ ☆ ☆

Ten Dreams / Declarations:

1.
2.
3.
4.
5.
6.
7.
8.
9.
10.

The next step(s) I am taking today

Today's Date

Today I'm Grateful For

1.

2.

3.

4.

5.

Order of Priorities

1.

2.

3.

4.

5.

☆ ☆ ☆ ☆ ☆

☆ ☆ ☆ ☆ ☆

☆ ☆ ☆ ☆ ☆

☆ ☆ ☆ ☆ ☆

☆ ☆ ☆ ☆ ☆

Ten Dreams / Declarations:

1.

2.

3.

4.

5.

6.

7.

8.

9.

10.

The next step(s) I am taking today

Today's Date

Today I'm Grateful For

1.

2.

3.

4.

5.

Order of Priorities

1.

2.

3.

4.

5.

How did I do Yesterday?

☆ ☆ ☆ ☆ ☆

☆ ☆ ☆ ☆ ☆

☆ ☆ ☆ ☆ ☆

☆ ☆ ☆ ☆ ☆

☆ ☆ ☆ ☆ ☆

Ten Dreams / Declarations:

1.

2.

3.

4.

5.

6.

7.

8.

9.

10.

The next step(s) I am taking today

Today I'm Grateful For

1.

2.

3.

4.

5.

Order of Priorities

1.

2.

3.

4.

5.

How did I do Yesterday?

☆ ☆ ☆ ☆ ☆

☆ ☆ ☆ ☆ ☆

☆ ☆ ☆ ☆ ☆

☆ ☆ ☆ ☆ ☆

☆ ☆ ☆ ☆ ☆

Ten Dreams / Declarations:

1.

2.

3.

4.

5.

6.

7.

8.

9.

10.

The next step(s) I am taking today

Today's Date

Today I'm Grateful For

1.
2.
3.
4.
5.

Order of Priorities

1.
2.
3.
4.
5.

How did I do Yesterday?

☆☆☆☆☆
☆☆☆☆☆
☆☆☆☆☆
☆☆☆☆☆
☆☆☆☆☆

Ten Dreams / Declarations:

1.
2.
3.
4.
5.
6.
7.
8.
9.
10.

The next step(s) I am taking today

Today's Date

Today I'm Grateful For

1.

2.

3.

4.

5.

Order of Priorities

How did I
do Yesterday?

1. ☆ ☆ ☆ ☆ ☆

2. ☆ ☆ ☆ ☆ ☆

3. ☆ ☆ ☆ ☆ ☆

4. ☆ ☆ ☆ ☆ ☆

5. ☆ ☆ ☆ ☆ ☆

Ten Dreams / Declarations:

1.

2.

3.

4.

5.

6.

7.

8.

9.

10.

The next step(s) I am taking today

Today I'm Grateful For	Order of Priorities	How did I do Yesterday?
1.	1.	☆ ☆ ☆ ☆ ☆
2.	2.	☆ ☆ ☆ ☆ ☆
3.	3.	☆ ☆ ☆ ☆ ☆
4.	4.	☆ ☆ ☆ ☆ ☆
5.	5.	☆ ☆ ☆ ☆ ☆

Ten Dreams / Declarations:

1.

2.

3.

4.

5.

6.

7.

8.

9.

10.

The next step(s) I am taking today

Today's Date

Today I'm Grateful For	Order of Priorities	How did I do Yesterday?
1.	1.	☆ ☆ ☆ ☆ ☆
2.	2.	☆ ☆ ☆ ☆ ☆
3.	3.	☆ ☆ ☆ ☆ ☆
4.	4.	☆ ☆ ☆ ☆ ☆
5.	5.	☆ ☆ ☆ ☆ ☆

Ten Dreams / Declarations:

1.

2.

3.

4.

5.

6.

7.

8.

9.

10.

The next step(s) I am taking today

Today's Date

Today I'm Grateful For	Order of Priorities	How did I do Yesterday?

Today I'm Grateful For	Order of Priorities	How did I do Yesterday?
1.	1.	☆ ☆ ☆ ☆ ☆
2.	2.	☆ ☆ ☆ ☆ ☆
3.	3.	☆ ☆ ☆ ☆ ☆
4.	4.	☆ ☆ ☆ ☆ ☆
5.	5.	☆ ☆ ☆ ☆ ☆

Ten Dreams / Declarations:

1.

2.

3.

4.

5.

6.

7.

8.

9.

10.

The next step(s) I am taking today

Today's Date

Today I'm Grateful For

1.
2.
3.
4.
5.

Order of Priorities

1.
2.
3.
4.
5.

How did I
do Yesterday?

☆ ☆ ☆ ☆ ☆
☆ ☆ ☆ ☆ ☆
☆ ☆ ☆ ☆ ☆
☆ ☆ ☆ ☆ ☆
☆ ☆ ☆ ☆ ☆

Ten Dreams / Declarations:

1.
2.
3.
4.
5.
6.
7.
8.
9.
10.

The next step(s) I am taking today

Today I'm Grateful For

1.

2.

3.

4.

5.

Order of Priorities

1.

2.

3.

4.

5.

How did I do Yesterday?

☆ ☆ ☆ ☆ ☆

☆ ☆ ☆ ☆ ☆

☆ ☆ ☆ ☆ ☆

☆ ☆ ☆ ☆ ☆

☆ ☆ ☆ ☆ ☆

Ten Dreams / Declarations:

1.

2.

3.

4.

5.

6.

7.

8.

9.

10.

The next step(s) I am taking today

Today's Date

Today I'm Grateful For	Order of Priorities	How did I do Yesterday?
1.	1.	☆ ☆ ☆ ☆ ☆
2.	2.	☆ ☆ ☆ ☆ ☆
3.	3.	☆ ☆ ☆ ☆ ☆
4.	4.	☆ ☆ ☆ ☆ ☆
5.	5.	☆ ☆ ☆ ☆ ☆

Ten Dreams / Declarations:

1.

2.

3.

4.

5.

6.

7.

8.

9.

10.

The next step(s) I am taking today

Today's Date

Today I'm Grateful For

1.

2.

3.

4.

5.

Order of Priorities

1.

2.

3.

4.

5.

How did I do Yesterday?

☆ ☆ ☆ ☆ ☆

☆ ☆ ☆ ☆ ☆

☆ ☆ ☆ ☆ ☆

☆ ☆ ☆ ☆ ☆

☆ ☆ ☆ ☆ ☆

Ten Dreams / Declarations:

1.

2.

3.

4.

5.

6.

7.

8.

9.

10.

The next step(s) I am taking today

Today's Date

Today I'm Grateful For

1.
2.
3.
4.
5.

Order of Priorities

1.
2.
3.
4.
5.

How did I do Yesterday?

☆ ☆ ☆ ☆ ☆
☆ ☆ ☆ ☆ ☆
☆ ☆ ☆ ☆ ☆
☆ ☆ ☆ ☆ ☆
☆ ☆ ☆ ☆ ☆

Ten Dreams / Declarations:

1.

2.

3.

4.

5.

6.

7.

8.

9.

10.

The next step(s) I am taking today

Today's Date

Today I'm Grateful For

1.
2.
3.
4.
5.

Order of Priorities

1.
2.
3.
4.
5.

How did I do Yesterday?

☆ ☆ ☆ ☆ ☆
☆ ☆ ☆ ☆ ☆
☆ ☆ ☆ ☆ ☆
☆ ☆ ☆ ☆ ☆
☆ ☆ ☆ ☆ ☆

Ten Dreams / Declarations:

1.
2.
3.
4.
5.
6.
7.
8.
9.
10.

The next step[s] I am taking today

Today I'm Grateful For

1.

2.

3.

4.

5.

Order of Priorities

1.

2.

3.

4.

5.

How did I do Yesterday?

☆ ☆ ☆ ☆ ☆

☆ ☆ ☆ ☆ ☆

☆ ☆ ☆ ☆ ☆

☆ ☆ ☆ ☆ ☆

☆ ☆ ☆ ☆ ☆

Ten Dreams / Declarations:

1.

2.

3.

4.

5.

6.

7.

8.

9.

10.

The next step(s) I am taking today

Today I'm Grateful For

1.

2.

3.

4.

5.

Order of Priorities

1.

2.

3.

4.

5.

How did I
do Yesterday?

☆ ☆ ☆ ☆ ☆

☆ ☆ ☆ ☆ ☆

☆ ☆ ☆ ☆ ☆

☆ ☆ ☆ ☆ ☆

☆ ☆ ☆ ☆ ☆

Ten Dreams / Declarations:

1.

2.

3.

4.

5.

6.

7.

8.

9.

10.

The next step(s) I am taking today

Today's Date

Today I'm Grateful For	Order of Priorities	How did I do Yesterday?
1.	1.	☆ ☆ ☆ ☆ ☆
2.	2.	☆ ☆ ☆ ☆ ☆
3.	3.	☆ ☆ ☆ ☆ ☆
4.	4.	☆ ☆ ☆ ☆ ☆
5.	5.	☆ ☆ ☆ ☆ ☆

Ten Dreams / Declarations:

1.

2.

3.

4.

5.

6.

7.

8.

9.

10.

The next step[s] I am taking today

Today I'm Grateful For

1.

2.

3.

4.

5.

Order of Priorities

1.

2.

3.

4.

5.

How did I do Yesterday?

☆ ☆ ☆ ☆ ☆

☆ ☆ ☆ ☆ ☆

☆ ☆ ☆ ☆ ☆

☆ ☆ ☆ ☆ ☆

☆ ☆ ☆ ☆ ☆

Ten Dreams / Declarations:

1.

2.

3.

4.

5.

6.

7.

8.

9.

10.

The next step(s) I am taking today

Today's Date

Today I'm Grateful For

1.
2.
3.
4.
5.

Order of Priorities

	How did I do Yesterday?
1.	☆ ☆ ☆ ☆ ☆
2.	☆ ☆ ☆ ☆ ☆
3.	☆ ☆ ☆ ☆ ☆
4.	☆ ☆ ☆ ☆ ☆
5.	☆ ☆ ☆ ☆ ☆

Ten Dreams / Declarations:

1.
2.
3.
4.
5.
6.
7.
8.
9.
10.

The next step(s) I am taking today

Today I'm Grateful For	Order of Priorities	How did I do Yesterday?
1.	1.	☆ ☆ ☆ ☆ ☆
2.	2.	☆ ☆ ☆ ☆ ☆
3.	3.	☆ ☆ ☆ ☆ ☆
4.	4.	☆ ☆ ☆ ☆ ☆
5.	5.	☆ ☆ ☆ ☆ ☆

Ten Dreams / Declarations:

1.

2.

3.

4.

5.

6.

7.

8.

9.

10.

The next step(s) I am taking today

Today's Date

Today I'm Grateful For

1.
2.
3.
4.
5.

Order of Priorities

	How did I do Yesterday?
1.	☆ ☆ ☆ ☆ ☆
2.	☆ ☆ ☆ ☆ ☆
3.	☆ ☆ ☆ ☆ ☆
4.	☆ ☆ ☆ ☆ ☆
5.	☆ ☆ ☆ ☆ ☆

Ten Dreams / Declarations:

1.

2.

3.

4.

5.

6.

7.

8.

9.

10.

The next step(s) I am taking today

Today I'm Grateful For

Order of Priorities

How did I
do Yesterday?

1.   1.   ☆ ☆ ☆ ☆ ☆

2.   2.   ☆ ☆ ☆ ☆ ☆

3.   3.   ☆ ☆ ☆ ☆ ☆

4.   4.   ☆ ☆ ☆ ☆ ☆

5.   5.   ☆ ☆ ☆ ☆ ☆

Ten Dreams / Declarations:

1.

2.

3.

4.

5.

6.

7.

8.

9.

10.

The next step[s] I am taking today

Today's Date

Today I'm Grateful For

1.
2.
3.
4.
5.

Order of Priorities

How did I
do Yesterday?

1. ☆ ☆ ☆ ☆ ☆
2. ☆ ☆ ☆ ☆ ☆
3. ☆ ☆ ☆ ☆ ☆
4. ☆ ☆ ☆ ☆ ☆
5. ☆ ☆ ☆ ☆ ☆

Ten Dreams / Declarations:

1.

2.

3.

4.

5.

6.

7.

8.

9.

10.

The next step(s) I am taking today

Today I'm Grateful For

1.
2.
3.
4.
5.

Order of Priorities

1.
2.
3.
4.
5.

How did I
do Yesterday?

☆ ☆ ☆ ☆ ☆
☆ ☆ ☆ ☆ ☆
☆ ☆ ☆ ☆ ☆
☆ ☆ ☆ ☆ ☆
☆ ☆ ☆ ☆ ☆

Ten Dreams / Declarations:

1.
2.
3.
4.
5.
6.
7.
8.
9.
10.

The next step(s) I am taking today

Today's Date

Today I'm Grateful For

1.
2.
3.
4.
5.

Order of Priorities

1.
2.
3.
4.
5.

How did I do Yesterday?

☆ ☆ ☆ ☆ ☆
☆ ☆ ☆ ☆ ☆
☆ ☆ ☆ ☆ ☆
☆ ☆ ☆ ☆ ☆
☆ ☆ ☆ ☆ ☆

Ten Dreams / Declarations:

1.

2.

3.

4.

5.

6.

7.

8.

9.

10.

The next step(s) I am taking today

Today I'm Grateful For

1.
2.
3.
4.
5.

Order of Priorities

1.
2.
3.
4.
5.

How did I do Yesterday?

☆ ☆ ☆ ☆ ☆
☆ ☆ ☆ ☆ ☆
☆ ☆ ☆ ☆ ☆
☆ ☆ ☆ ☆ ☆
☆ ☆ ☆ ☆ ☆

Ten Dreams / Declarations:

1.
2.
3.
4.
5.
6.
7.
8.
9.
10.

The next step(s) I am taking today

Today's Date

Today I'm Grateful For

1.

2.

3.

4.

5.

Order of Priorities

1.

2.

3.

4.

5.

How did I do Yesterday?

☆ ☆ ☆ ☆ ☆

☆ ☆ ☆ ☆ ☆

☆ ☆ ☆ ☆ ☆

☆ ☆ ☆ ☆ ☆

☆ ☆ ☆ ☆ ☆

Ten Dreams / Declarations:

1.

2.

3.

4.

5.

6.

7.

8.

9.

10.

The next step(s) I am taking today

Today's Date

Today I'm Grateful For

1.

2.

3.

4.

5.

Order of Priorities

1.

2.

3.

4.

5.

How did I do Yesterday?

☆ ☆ ☆ ☆ ☆

☆ ☆ ☆ ☆ ☆

☆ ☆ ☆ ☆ ☆

☆ ☆ ☆ ☆ ☆

☆ ☆ ☆ ☆ ☆

Ten Dreams / Declarations:

1.

2.

3.

4.

5.

6.

7.

8.

9.

10.

The next step(s) I am taking today

Today I'm Grateful For

1.
2.
3.
4.
5.

Order of Priorities

1.
2.
3.
4.
5.

How did I do Yesterday?

☆ ☆ ☆ ☆ ☆
☆ ☆ ☆ ☆ ☆
☆ ☆ ☆ ☆ ☆
☆ ☆ ☆ ☆ ☆
☆ ☆ ☆ ☆ ☆

Ten Dreams / Declarations:

1.

2.

3.

4.

5.

6.

7.

8.

9.

10.

The next step(s) I am taking today

Today I'm Grateful For

1.

2.

3.

4.

5.

Order of Priorities

1.

2.

3.

4.

5.

How did I do Yesterday?

☆ ☆ ☆ ☆ ☆

☆ ☆ ☆ ☆ ☆

☆ ☆ ☆ ☆ ☆

☆ ☆ ☆ ☆ ☆

☆ ☆ ☆ ☆ ☆

Ten Dreams / Declarations:

1.

2.

3.

4.

5.

6.

7.

8.

9.

10.

The next step(s) I am taking today

Today's Date

Today I'm Grateful For

1.

2.

3.

4.

5.

Order of Priorities

1.

2.

3.

4.

5.

How did I
do Yesterday?

☆ ☆ ☆ ☆ ☆

☆ ☆ ☆ ☆ ☆

☆ ☆ ☆ ☆ ☆

☆ ☆ ☆ ☆ ☆

☆ ☆ ☆ ☆ ☆

Ten Dreams / Declarations:

1.

2.

3.

4.

5.

6.

7.

8.

9.

10.

The next step(s) I am taking today

Today's Date

Today I'm Grateful For

1.

2.

3.

4.

5.

Order of Priorities

1.

2.

3.

4.

5.

How did I do Yesterday?

☆ ☆ ☆ ☆ ☆

☆ ☆ ☆ ☆ ☆

☆ ☆ ☆ ☆ ☆

☆ ☆ ☆ ☆ ☆

☆ ☆ ☆ ☆ ☆

Ten Dreams / Declarations:

1.

2.

3.

4.

5.

6.

7.

8.

9.

10.

The next step(s) I am taking today

Today's Date

Today I'm Grateful For	Order of Priorities	How did I do Yesterday?
1.	1.	☆ ☆ ☆ ☆ ☆
2.	2.	☆ ☆ ☆ ☆ ☆
3.	3.	☆ ☆ ☆ ☆ ☆
4.	4.	☆ ☆ ☆ ☆ ☆
5.	5.	☆ ☆ ☆ ☆ ☆

Ten Dreams / Declarations:

1.

2.

3.

4.

5.

6.

7.

8.

9.

10.

The next step(s) I am taking today

Today's Date

Today I'm Grateful For

	Order of Priorities	How did I do Yesterday?
1.	1.	☆ ☆ ☆ ☆ ☆
2.	2.	☆ ☆ ☆ ☆ ☆
3.	3.	☆ ☆ ☆ ☆ ☆
4.	4.	☆ ☆ ☆ ☆ ☆
5.	5.	☆ ☆ ☆ ☆ ☆

Ten Dreams / Declarations:

1.

2.

3.

4.

5.

6.

7.

8.

9.

10.

The next step(s) I am taking today

Today's Date

Today I'm Grateful For	Order of Priorities	How did I do Yesterday?
1.	1.	☆ ☆ ☆ ☆ ☆
2.	2.	☆ ☆ ☆ ☆ ☆
3.	3.	☆ ☆ ☆ ☆ ☆
4.	4.	☆ ☆ ☆ ☆ ☆
5.	5.	☆ ☆ ☆ ☆ ☆

Ten Dreams / Declarations:

1.

2.

3.

4.

5.

6.

7.

8.

9.

10.

The next step(s) I am taking today

Today I'm Grateful For

1.
2.
3.
4.
5.

Order of Priorities

1.
2.
3.
4.
5.

How did I do Yesterday?

☆ ☆ ☆ ☆ ☆
☆ ☆ ☆ ☆ ☆
☆ ☆ ☆ ☆ ☆
☆ ☆ ☆ ☆ ☆
☆ ☆ ☆ ☆ ☆

Ten Dreams / Declarations:

1.
2.
3.
4.
5.
6.
7.
8.
9.
10.

The next step(s) I am taking today

Today's Date

Today I'm Grateful For

1.

2.

3.

4.

5.

Order of Priorities

1.

2.

3.

4.

5.

How did I do Yesterday?

☆ ☆ ☆ ☆ ☆

☆ ☆ ☆ ☆ ☆

☆ ☆ ☆ ☆ ☆

☆ ☆ ☆ ☆ ☆

☆ ☆ ☆ ☆ ☆

Ten Dreams / Declarations:

1.

2.

3.

4.

5.

6.

7.

8.

9.

10.

The next step(s) I am taking today

Today I'm Grateful For	Order of Priorities	How did I do Yesterday?
1.	1.	☆ ☆ ☆ ☆ ☆
2.	2.	☆ ☆ ☆ ☆ ☆
3.	3.	☆ ☆ ☆ ☆ ☆
4.	4.	☆ ☆ ☆ ☆ ☆
5.	5.	☆ ☆ ☆ ☆ ☆

Ten Dreams / Declarations:

1.

2.

3.

4.

5.

6.

7.

8.

9.

10.

The next step(s) I am taking today

Today I'm Grateful For

1.

2.

3.

4.

5.

Order of Priorities

1.

2.

3.

4.

5.

How did I do Yesterday?

☆ ☆ ☆ ☆ ☆

☆ ☆ ☆ ☆ ☆

☆ ☆ ☆ ☆ ☆

☆ ☆ ☆ ☆ ☆

☆ ☆ ☆ ☆ ☆

Ten Dreams / Declarations:

1.

2.

3.

4.

5.

6.

7.

8.

9.

10.

The next step(s) I am taking today

Today's Date

Today I'm Grateful For

Order of Priorities

How did I
do Yesterday?

1.

2.

3.

4.

5.

1. ☆ ☆ ☆ ☆ ☆

2. ☆ ☆ ☆ ☆ ☆

3. ☆ ☆ ☆ ☆ ☆

4. ☆ ☆ ☆ ☆ ☆

5. ☆ ☆ ☆ ☆ ☆

Ten Dreams / Declarations:

1.

2.

3.

4.

5.

6.

7.

8.

9.

10.

The next step(s) I am taking today

Today I'm Grateful For

1.

2.

3.

4.

5.

Order of Priorities

1.

2.

3.

4.

5.

How did I do Yesterday?

☆ ☆ ☆ ☆ ☆

☆ ☆ ☆ ☆ ☆

☆ ☆ ☆ ☆ ☆

☆ ☆ ☆ ☆ ☆

☆ ☆ ☆ ☆ ☆

Ten Dreams / Declarations:

1.

2.

3.

4.

5.

6.

7.

8.

9.

10.

The next step(s) I am taking today

Today's Date

Today I'm Grateful For	Order of Priorities	How did I do Yesterday?
1.	1.	☆ ☆ ☆ ☆ ☆
2.	2.	☆ ☆ ☆ ☆ ☆
3.	3.	☆ ☆ ☆ ☆ ☆
4.	4.	☆ ☆ ☆ ☆ ☆
5.	5.	☆ ☆ ☆ ☆ ☆

Ten Dreams / Declarations:

1.

2.

3.

4.

5.

6.

7.

8.

9.

10.

The next step(s) I am taking today

Today's Date

Today I'm Grateful For

1.

2.

3.

4.

5.

Order of Priorities

1.

2.

3.

4.

5.

How did I do Yesterday?

☆ ☆ ☆ ☆ ☆

☆ ☆ ☆ ☆ ☆

☆ ☆ ☆ ☆ ☆

☆ ☆ ☆ ☆ ☆

☆ ☆ ☆ ☆ ☆

Ten Dreams / Declarations:

1.

2.

3.

4.

5.

6.

7.

8.

9.

10.

The next step(s) I am taking today

Today I'm Grateful For

1.
2.
3.
4.
5.

Order of Priorities

1.
2.
3.
4.
5.

How did I do Yesterday?

☆ ☆ ☆ ☆ ☆
☆ ☆ ☆ ☆ ☆
☆ ☆ ☆ ☆ ☆
☆ ☆ ☆ ☆ ☆
☆ ☆ ☆ ☆ ☆

Ten Dreams / Declarations:

1.
2.
3.
4.
5.
6.
7.
8.
9.
10.

The next step(s) I am taking today

Today I'm Grateful For

1.

2.

3.

4.

5.

Order of Priorities

1.

2.

3.

4.

5.

How did I do Yesterday?

☆ ☆ ☆ ☆ ☆

☆ ☆ ☆ ☆ ☆

☆ ☆ ☆ ☆ ☆

☆ ☆ ☆ ☆ ☆

☆ ☆ ☆ ☆ ☆

Ten Dreams / Declarations:

1.

2.

3.

4.

5.

6.

7.

8.

9.

10.

The next step(s) I am taking today

Today I'm Grateful For

Order of Priorities

1.

1.

☆ ☆ ☆ ☆ ☆

2.

2.

☆ ☆ ☆ ☆ ☆

3.

3.

☆ ☆ ☆ ☆ ☆

4.

4.

☆ ☆ ☆ ☆ ☆

5.

5.

☆ ☆ ☆ ☆ ☆

Ten Dreams / Declarations:

1.

2.

3.

4.

5.

6.

7.

8.

9.

10.

The next step(s) I am taking today

Today's Date

Today I'm Grateful For

1.
2.
3.
4.
5.

Order of Priorities

1.
2.
3.
4.
5.

How did I do Yesterday?

☆ ☆ ☆ ☆ ☆
☆ ☆ ☆ ☆ ☆
☆ ☆ ☆ ☆ ☆
☆ ☆ ☆ ☆ ☆
☆ ☆ ☆ ☆ ☆

Ten Dreams / Declarations:

1.

2.

3.

4.

5.

6.

7.

8.

9.

10.

The next step(s) I am taking today

Today's Date

Today I'm Grateful For

1.

2.

3.

4.

5.

Order of Priorities

1.

2.

3.

4.

5.

How did I do Yesterday?

☆ ☆ ☆ ☆ ☆

☆ ☆ ☆ ☆ ☆

☆ ☆ ☆ ☆ ☆

☆ ☆ ☆ ☆ ☆

☆ ☆ ☆ ☆ ☆

Ten Dreams / Declarations:

1.

2.

3.

4.

5.

6.

7.

8.

9.

10.

The next step(s) I am taking today

Today's Date

Today I'm Grateful For	Order of Priorities	How did I do Yesterday?
1.	1.	☆ ☆ ☆ ☆ ☆
2.	2.	☆ ☆ ☆ ☆ ☆
3.	3.	☆ ☆ ☆ ☆ ☆
4.	4.	☆ ☆ ☆ ☆ ☆
5.	5.	☆ ☆ ☆ ☆ ☆

Ten Dreams / Declarations:

1.

2.

3.

4.

5.

6.

7.

8.

9.

10.

The next step(s) I am taking today

Today I'm Grateful For	Order of Priorities	How did I do Yesterday?
1.	1.	☆ ☆ ☆ ☆ ☆
2.	2.	☆ ☆ ☆ ☆ ☆
3.	3.	☆ ☆ ☆ ☆ ☆
4.	4.	☆ ☆ ☆ ☆ ☆
5.	5.	☆ ☆ ☆ ☆ ☆

Ten Dreams / Declarations:

1.

2.

3.

4.

5.

6.

7.

8.

9.

10.

The next step(s) I am taking today

Today I'm Grateful For

1.

2.

3.

4.

5.

Order of Priorities

1.

2.

3.

4.

5.

How did I do Yesterday?

☆ ☆ ☆ ☆ ☆

☆ ☆ ☆ ☆ ☆

☆ ☆ ☆ ☆ ☆

☆ ☆ ☆ ☆ ☆

☆ ☆ ☆ ☆ ☆

Ten Dreams / Declarations:

1.

2.

3.

4.

5.

6.

7.

8.

9.

10.

The next step(s) I am taking today

Today I'm Grateful For

1.
2.
3.
4.
5.

Order of Priorities

1.
2.
3.
4.
5.

How did I do Yesterday?

☆ ☆ ☆ ☆ ☆
☆ ☆ ☆ ☆ ☆
☆ ☆ ☆ ☆ ☆
☆ ☆ ☆ ☆ ☆
☆ ☆ ☆ ☆ ☆

Ten Dreams / Declarations:

1.
2.
3.
4.
5.
6.
7.
8.
9.
10.

The next step(s) I am taking today

Today I'm Grateful For

1.

2.

3.

4.

5.

Order of Priorities

1.

2.

3.

4.

5.

How did I do Yesterday?

☆ ☆ ☆ ☆ ☆

☆ ☆ ☆ ☆ ☆

☆ ☆ ☆ ☆ ☆

☆ ☆ ☆ ☆ ☆

☆ ☆ ☆ ☆ ☆

Ten Dreams / Declarations:

1.

2.

3.

4.

5.

6.

7.

8.

9.

10.

The next step(s) I am taking today

Today I'm Grateful For

1.

2.

3.

4.

5.

Order of Priorities

1.

2.

3.

4.

5.

How did I do Yesterday?

☆ ☆ ☆ ☆ ☆

☆ ☆ ☆ ☆ ☆

☆ ☆ ☆ ☆ ☆

☆ ☆ ☆ ☆ ☆

☆ ☆ ☆ ☆ ☆

Ten Dreams / Declarations:

1.

2.

3.

4.

5.

6.

7.

8.

9.

10.

The next step(s) I am taking today

Today I'm Grateful For

Order of Priorities

How did I
do Yesterday?

1.

1. ☆ ☆ ☆ ☆ ☆

2.

2. ☆ ☆ ☆ ☆ ☆

3.

3. ☆ ☆ ☆ ☆ ☆

4.

4. ☆ ☆ ☆ ☆ ☆

5.

5. ☆ ☆ ☆ ☆ ☆

Ten Dreams / Declarations:

1.

2.

3.

4.

5.

6.

7.

8.

9.

10.

The next step(s) I am taking today

Today I'm Grateful For

1.

2.

3.

4.

5.

Order of Priorities

1.

2.

3.

4.

5.

How did I do Yesterday?

☆ ☆ ☆ ☆ ☆

☆ ☆ ☆ ☆ ☆

☆ ☆ ☆ ☆ ☆

☆ ☆ ☆ ☆ ☆

☆ ☆ ☆ ☆ ☆

Ten Dreams / Declarations:

1.

2.

3.

4.

5.

6.

7.

8.

9.

10.

The next step(s) I am taking today

Today's Date

Today I'm Grateful For

1.
2.
3.
4.
5.

Order of Priorities

1.
2.
3.
4.
5.

How did I do Yesterday?

☆ ☆ ☆ ☆ ☆
☆ ☆ ☆ ☆ ☆
☆ ☆ ☆ ☆ ☆
☆ ☆ ☆ ☆ ☆
☆ ☆ ☆ ☆ ☆

Ten Dreams / Declarations:

1.
2.
3.
4.
5.
6.
7.
8.
9.
10.

The next step(s) I am taking today

Today I'm Grateful For

1.

2.

3.

4.

5.

Order of Priorities

1.

2.

3.

4.

5.

How did I do Yesterday?

☆ ☆ ☆ ☆ ☆

☆ ☆ ☆ ☆ ☆

☆ ☆ ☆ ☆ ☆

☆ ☆ ☆ ☆ ☆

☆ ☆ ☆ ☆ ☆

Ten Dreams / Declarations:

1.

2.

3.

4.

5.

6.

7.

8.

9.

10.

The next step[s] I am taking today

Today's Date

Today I'm Grateful For

1.

2.

3.

4.

5.

Order of Priorities

1.

2.

3.

4.

5.

How did I
do Yesterday?

☆ ☆ ☆ ☆ ☆

☆ ☆ ☆ ☆ ☆

☆ ☆ ☆ ☆ ☆

☆ ☆ ☆ ☆ ☆

☆ ☆ ☆ ☆ ☆

Ten Dreams / Declarations:

1.

2.

3.

4.

5.

6.

7.

8.

9.

10.

The next step(s) I am taking today

Today I'm Grateful For

1.

2.

3.

4.

5.

Order of Priorities

1.

2.

3.

4.

5.

How did I do Yesterday?

☆ ☆ ☆ ☆ ☆

☆ ☆ ☆ ☆ ☆

☆ ☆ ☆ ☆ ☆

☆ ☆ ☆ ☆ ☆

☆ ☆ ☆ ☆ ☆

Ten Dreams / Declarations:

1.

2.

3.

4.

5.

6.

7.

8.

9.

10.

The next step(s) I am taking today

Today I'm Grateful For

1.

2.

3.

4.

5.

Order of Priorities

1.

2.

3.

4.

5.

How did I do Yesterday?

☆ ☆ ☆ ☆ ☆

☆ ☆ ☆ ☆ ☆

☆ ☆ ☆ ☆ ☆

☆ ☆ ☆ ☆ ☆

☆ ☆ ☆ ☆ ☆

Ten Dreams / Declarations:

1.

2.

3.

4.

5.

6.

7.

8.

9.

10.

The next step(s) I am taking today

Today I'm Grateful For	Order of Priorities	How did I do Yesterday?
		☆ ☆ ☆ ☆ ☆
1.	1.	
		☆ ☆ ☆ ☆ ☆
2.	2.	
		☆ ☆ ☆ ☆ ☆
3.	3.	
		☆ ☆ ☆ ☆ ☆
4.	4.	
		☆ ☆ ☆ ☆ ☆
5.	5.	

Ten Dreams / Declarations:

1.

2.

3.

4.

5.

6.

7.

8.

9.

10.

The next step(s) I am taking today

Today's Date

Today I'm Grateful For

1.

2.

3.

4.

5.

Order of Priorities

1.

2.

3.

4.

5.

How did I do Yesterday?

☆ ☆ ☆ ☆ ☆

☆ ☆ ☆ ☆ ☆

☆ ☆ ☆ ☆ ☆

☆ ☆ ☆ ☆ ☆

☆ ☆ ☆ ☆ ☆

Ten Dreams / Declarations:

1.

2.

3.

4.

5.

6.

7.

8.

9.

10.

The next step(s) I am taking today

Today I'm Grateful For	Order of Priorities	How did I do Yesterday?
1.	1.	☆ ☆ ☆ ☆ ☆
2.	2.	☆ ☆ ☆ ☆ ☆
3.	3.	☆ ☆ ☆ ☆ ☆
4.	4.	☆ ☆ ☆ ☆ ☆
5.	5.	☆ ☆ ☆ ☆ ☆

Ten Dreams / Declarations:

1.

2.

3.

4.

5.

6.

7.

8.

9.

10.

The next step(s) I am taking today

Today's Date

Today I'm Grateful For

1.
2.
3.
4.
5.

Order of Priorities

1.
2.
3.
4.
5.

How did I do Yesterday?

☆ ☆ ☆ ☆ ☆
☆ ☆ ☆ ☆ ☆
☆ ☆ ☆ ☆ ☆
☆ ☆ ☆ ☆ ☆
☆ ☆ ☆ ☆ ☆

Ten Dreams / Declarations:

1.

2.

3.

4.

5.

6.

7.

8.

9.

10.

The next step(s) I am taking today

Today's Date

Today I'm Grateful For	Order of Priorities	How did I do Yesterday?
		☆ ☆ ☆ ☆ ☆
1.	1.	
		☆ ☆ ☆ ☆ ☆
2.	2.	
		☆ ☆ ☆ ☆ ☆
3.	3.	
		☆ ☆ ☆ ☆ ☆
4.	4.	
		☆ ☆ ☆ ☆ ☆
5.	5.	

Ten Dreams / Declarations:

1.

2.

3.

4.

5.

6.

7.

8.

9.

10.

The next step(s) I am taking today

Today's Date

Today I'm Grateful For

1.
2.
3.
4.
5.

Order of Priorities

1.
2.
3.
4.
5.

How did I do Yesterday?

☆ ☆ ☆ ☆ ☆
☆ ☆ ☆ ☆ ☆
☆ ☆ ☆ ☆ ☆
☆ ☆ ☆ ☆ ☆
☆ ☆ ☆ ☆ ☆

Ten Dreams / Declarations:

1.

2.

3.

4.

5.

6.

7.

8.

9.

10.

The next step(s) I am taking today

Today I'm Grateful For	Order of Priorities	How did I do Yesterday?
		☆ ☆ ☆ ☆ ☆
1.	1.	
		☆ ☆ ☆ ☆ ☆
2.	2.	
		☆ ☆ ☆ ☆ ☆
3.	3.	
		☆ ☆ ☆ ☆ ☆
4.	4.	
		☆ ☆ ☆ ☆ ☆
5.	5.	

Ten Dreams / Declarations:

1.

2.

3.

4.

5.

6.

7.

8.

9.

10.

The next step[s] I am taking today

Today's Date

Today I'm Grateful For

1.

2.

3.

4.

5.

Order of Priorities

1.

2.

3.

4.

5.

How did I
do Yesterday?

☆ ☆ ☆ ☆ ☆

☆ ☆ ☆ ☆ ☆

☆ ☆ ☆ ☆ ☆

☆ ☆ ☆ ☆ ☆

☆ ☆ ☆ ☆ ☆

Ten Dreams / Declarations:

1.

2.

3.

4.

5.

6.

7.

8.

9.

10.

The next step(s) I am taking today

Today I'm Grateful For	Order of Priorities	How did I do Yesterday?
1.	1.	☆ ☆ ☆ ☆ ☆
2.	2.	☆ ☆ ☆ ☆ ☆
3.	3.	☆ ☆ ☆ ☆ ☆
4.	4.	☆ ☆ ☆ ☆ ☆
5.	5.	☆ ☆ ☆ ☆ ☆

Ten Dreams / Declarations:

1.

2.

3.

4.

5.

6.

7.

8.

9.

10.

The next step(s) I am taking today

Today I'm Grateful For

1.
2.
3.
4.
5.

Order of Priorities

1.
2.
3.
4.
5.

How did I do Yesterday?

☆ ☆ ☆ ☆ ☆
☆ ☆ ☆ ☆ ☆
☆ ☆ ☆ ☆ ☆
☆ ☆ ☆ ☆ ☆
☆ ☆ ☆ ☆ ☆

Ten Dreams / Declarations:

1.

2.

3.

4.

5.

6.

7.

8.

9.

10.

The next step(s) I am taking today

Today's Date

Today I'm Grateful For	Order of Priorities	How did I do Yesterday?

Today I'm Grateful For

1.

2.

3.

4.

5.

Order of Priorities

1. ☆ ☆ ☆ ☆ ☆

2. ☆ ☆ ☆ ☆ ☆

3. ☆ ☆ ☆ ☆ ☆

4. ☆ ☆ ☆ ☆ ☆

5. ☆ ☆ ☆ ☆ ☆

Ten Dreams / Declarations:

1.

2.

3.

4.

5.

6.

7.

8.

9.

10.

The next step(s) I am taking today

Today I'm Grateful For

1.

2.

3.

4.

5.

Order of Priorities

1.

2.

3.

4.

5.

How did I do Yesterday?

☆ ☆ ☆ ☆ ☆

☆ ☆ ☆ ☆ ☆

☆ ☆ ☆ ☆ ☆

☆ ☆ ☆ ☆ ☆

☆ ☆ ☆ ☆ ☆

Ten Dreams / Declarations:

1.

2.

3.

4.

5.

6.

7.

8.

9.

10.

The next step(s) I am taking today

Today I'm Grateful For

1.
2.
3.
4.
5.

Order of Priorities

1.
2.
3.
4.
5.

How did I do Yesterday?

☆ ☆ ☆ ☆ ☆
☆ ☆ ☆ ☆ ☆
☆ ☆ ☆ ☆ ☆
☆ ☆ ☆ ☆ ☆
☆ ☆ ☆ ☆ ☆

Ten Dreams / Declarations:

1.
2.
3.
4.
5.
6.
7.
8.
9.
10.

The next step[s] I am taking today

Today's Date

Today I'm Grateful For

1.
2.
3.
4.
5.

Order of Priorities

1.
2.
3.
4.
5.

How did I
do Yesterday?

☆ ☆ ☆ ☆ ☆
☆ ☆ ☆ ☆ ☆
☆ ☆ ☆ ☆ ☆
☆ ☆ ☆ ☆ ☆
☆ ☆ ☆ ☆ ☆

Ten Dreams / Declarations:

1.

2.

3.

4.

5.

6.

7.

8.

9.

10.

The next step(s) I am taking today

156 Wildfire Daily Journal

You did it! We are proud of you. You just completed your first 2x5=10 journal. We are confident that the combination of gratitude and ordering of priorities will accelerate you living out your dreams! We want to challenge you to keep running towards your dreams. Grow them, expand them, refine them, and achieve them. Fight for what truly matters in your life. Do not let something of a lesser priority dominate your life, consuming the resources you could be spending on what is truly important to you.

You are off to a great start and this is only the beginning! We hope that this journal has become part of your daily routine and that it helps you stay focused on the dreams, goals and priorities you have for your life. The point of this practice is to **filter** your life through your order of priorities and to empower you to **intentionally** achieve your dreams, and you are nailing it.

> "I don't know about you, but I'm running hard for the finish line. I'm giving it everything I've got. No sloppy living for me! I'm staying alert and in top condition. I'm not going to get caught napping, telling everyone else all about it and then missing out myself."
>
> ~ 1 Corinthians 9:26-27 (MSG)

Don't allow the journey to end here; keep your journal going and watch your dreams become a reality!

God bless you,
Bill and Stephanie

To re-order the Wildfire Daily Journal and for additional tools and resources to equip you on your journey, be sure to visit

wildfire-leadership.com

About The Authors

Bill and Stephanie Lammers have been married 22 years and have four children; Will, Joseph, Adelynn, and Josiah. As a couple, Bill and Stephanie love encouraging leaders to take the next steps to growth, while at the same time remaining humble, teachable, and eager to keep learning and developing themselves. They want to be a catalyst for change and their heart as leaders is to leave people better than they found them. They take a genuine interest in people and have a strong desire to help activate passions and gifts in leaders.

Bill has been a business leader for over 20 years and currently serves as CEO of Rooted Advisors and the Defiance Dream Center, and is the Executive Pastor at Xperience Church. He is a visionary with the gift of being able to see the bigger picture and has led four separate company turnarounds by investing in, developing, and coaching high capacity leaders and placing them in positions to thrive. He holds dual Masters Degrees in business administration and organizational leadership, an engineering degree, and is a certified John Maxwell coach.

Stephanie was a cardiac nurse for 20+ years. She has homeschooled her children, while simultaneously speaking at women's events, and leading parenting and marriage classes. Stephanie has co-authored multiple women devotionals and published a bible study. As a certified DISC instructor, Stephanie facilitates programs for organizations and executive teams and coaches women one-on-one. She is passionate about coming alongside and equipping women to lead fulfilling lives by helping them discover true joy as they learn to lead in their lane.

Made in the
USA
Middletown, DE